HENRY AND THE ELEPHANT

by

The Rev. W. Awdry
and
Christopher Awdry

with illustrations by
C. Reginald Dalby
and
Clive Spong

GROLIER

Henry and the Elephant

HENRY and Gordon were lonely when Thomas left the yard to run his Branch Line. They missed him very much.

They had more work to do. They couldn't wait in the shed till it was time, and find their coaches at the platform; they had to fetch them. They didn't like that.

Edward sometimes did odd jobs, and so did James, but James soon started grumbling too. The Fat Controller kindly gave Henry and Gordon new coats of paint (Henry chose green), but they still grumbled dreadfully.

"We get no rest, we get no rest," they complained as they clanked about the yard; but the coaches only laughed.

"You're lazy and slack, you're lazy and slack," they answered in their quiet, rude way.

But when a Circus came to town, the engines forgot they were tired. They all wanted to shunt the special trucks and coaches.

They were dreadfully jealous of James when the Fat Controller told him to pull the train when the Circus went away.

However, they soon forgot about the animals as they had plenty of work to do.

One morning Henry was told to take some workmen to a tunnel which was blocked.

He grumbled away to find two trucks to carry the workmen and their tools.

"Pushing trucks! Pushing trucks!" he muttered in a sulky sort of way.

They stopped outside the tunnel, and tried to look through it, but it was quite dark; no daylight shone from the other end.

The workmen took their tools and went inside.

Suddenly with a shout they all ran out looking frightened.

"We went to the block and started to dig, but it grunted and moved," they said.

"Rubbish," said the foreman.

"It's not rubbish, it's big and alive; we're not going in there again."

"Right," said the foreman, "I'll ride in a truck and Henry shall push it out."

"Wheeeesh," said Henry unhappily. He hated tunnels (he had been shut up in one once), but this was worse; something big and alive was inside.

"Peep peep peep pip pip pee—eep!" he whistled, "I don't want to go in!"

"Neither do I," said his driver, "but we must clear the line."

"Oh dear! Oh dear!" puffed Henry as they slowly advanced into the darkness.

B U M P————!!!!

Henry's driver shut off steam at once.

"Help! Help! we're going back," wailed Henry, and slowly moving out into the daylight came first Henry, then the trucks, and last of all, pushing hard and rather cross, came a large elephant.

"Well I never did!" said the foreman. "It's an elephant from the Circus."

Henry's driver put on his brakes, and a man ran to telephone for the keeper.

The elephant stopped pushing and came towards them. They gave him some sandwiches and cake, so he forgot he was cross and remembered he was hungry. He drank three buckets of water without stopping, and was just going to drink another when Henry let off steam.

The elephant jumped, and "hoo——oosh", he squirted the water over Henry by mistake.

Poor Henry!

When the keeper came, the workmen rode home happily in the trucks, laughing at their adventure, but Henry was very cross.

"An elephant pushed me! An elephant hooshed me!" he hissed.

He was sulky all day, and his coaches had an uncomfortable time.

In the shed he told Gordon and James about the elephant, and I am sorry to say that instead of laughing and telling him not to be silly, they looked sad and said:

"You poor engine, you have been badly treated."

Fire-Engine

"'FLYING SCOTSMAN' and my brothers were all green," explained Gordon one night in the shed. "It was all very well in its way, but now I prefer my blue. It makes me different, you see, and that's very suitable for an important engine like me."

"The engines on oor auld line used to be blue," remembered Donald, "but nae sae dark as we are. Dougie and me never were though – we had to be black, sae blue makes a nice change."

"I like my green too," agreed Henry. "I'd hate to be red like James. People would think I was a fire-engine."

"At least people can see me coming," retorted James. "I don't disappear into the background like some engines I could mention. If it wasn't for the noise, you'd need a yellow and black front like Mavis."

Henry's protests were drowned in the laughter of the other engines, and he went to sleep wondering how to pay James out.

Henry was still cross next morning.

"What can be wrong? What can be wrong?" wondered the coaches anxiously as Henry pulled noisily away from the Big Station.

"Do come along, do come along," Henry snorted impatiently.

They had a fast run, but it didn't improve Henry's temper. He bumped the coaches when they reached the end of the line, and again when he backed on to them for the return journey. He simmered angrily while the fireman fastened the coupling.

No one noticed a rattle from beneath Henry's footplate as he snorted away, and soon the train was running well.

"Hurry, hurry, hurry," puffed Henry. Faster and faster they went. At last Henry began to feel better.

Suddenly he heard a crack from below his cab.

"Look out!" shouted the driver. He applied the brakes while the fireman scrambled forward to the footplate. He was just in time. Both men watched in horror as a widening gap opened between Henry and his tender.

Henry stopped as soon as he could. The automatic brake halted his tender and the train some way behind.

"We must drop Henry's fire," said the driver urgently. "It will be dangerous to let him boil dry now that we can't get more water from the tender."

The fireman agreed.

"Sorry, old boy," he said to Henry. "Just when we'd got it going nicely too. But if you hadn't banged about so much you wouldn't have broken your tender coupling."

While the fireman dealt with the fire, the driver went back to tell the signalman what had happened. When he returned he found Henry completely hidden in a huge cloud of black smoke, which billowed from beneath his cab.

The fireman emerged, choking.

"Henry's fire set the sleepers alight," he spluttered. "You stay here—I'm going to phone the fire-brigade."

The driver eased Henry clear of the blaze, and then Edward came to take his train on. Henry felt most uncomfortable.

Workmen made Henry a temporary coupling. They rejoined him to his tender, and then the driver and fireman lit a new fire and drove him gently home.

Edward, who had of course seen everything, told the others. They were careful what they talked about that night.

As for Henry, he was touchy on the subject of fires for some time afterwards. But James was quick to notice that from then on Henry stopped making rude remarks about the colour of fire-engines.